KIKI

KIKI

A Cuban Boy's Adventures in America

Hilda Perera

Translation by
Warren Hampton and Hilda González S.

The Pickering Press, Inc.
Coconut Grove, Florida

The Pickering Press, Inc.
Coconut Grove, Florida
Distributed by The Talman Company

Library of Congress Cataloging in Publication Data
Perera, Hilda, 1926-
  [Kike. English]
  Kiki / Hilda Perera ; translation by Warren
Hampton, Hilda
González S. ; [cover and illustrations by Mathieu
Nuygen].
    p. cm.
  Translation of : Kike.
  Summary: In the early 1960s eight-year-old Kiki
leaves Cuba to escape the Castro regime and tries
to adjust in two very different foster homes in
Florida, first with a poor family in the Everglades
and then with a wealthy family in Miami.
  ISBN 0-940495-24-4 (paper) : $10.95
  [1. Refugees--Fiction. 2. Cuban Americans--Fiction.
3. Foster home care--Fiction. 4. Everglades (Fla.)--
Fiction. 5. Florida--Fiction.] I. Nuygen, Mathieu,
ill. II. Title.
PZ7.P4249Ki 1992
[Fic]--dc20   92-11954
                                              CIP
                                              AC

Cover and illustrations by Mathieu Nuygen

Contents

Kiki,
as depicted on the cover of this book,
is modeled after a ward of
the Children's Home Society
of South Florida.

I

Good-Bye Cuba. Hello Miami.

"*Buenas tardes, señoras y señores.* Good evening ladies and gentlemen, this is Pan American Airways Flight 102 from Havana to Miami."

I couldn't see who said it, and nobody ever called me *señor*, but I answered back, "*Buenas tardes.*"

"Dummy!" my brother laughed at me.

Little red lights went on at the wing tip of the plane, and the voice in Spanish returned.

"Fasten your seatbelts, please."

I buckled up even though I was jittery and had to go to the bathroom. It always happened when I got scared, so I tried to put my mind on something else. First I started pressing the lid of a small metal box on the arm of the seat. Nothing happened. Then I pressed some more and it popped open, spilling ashes and cigarette butts all over me.

I noticed the round button to tilt the seat back. I pressed it and stretched my legs. I tried again. Since I was also kicking the seat in front of me, the lady sitting there turned and snapped, "Would you please sit still?"

I looked up and saw a round metal thing with a tiny hole. I stood on the seat to reach it. When I opened the hole all the way, a nice cool blast of air rushed in, but it made the lady sneeze.

"Cut it out! Will you?" my brother Tony demanded.

Then I opened the slip of paper Mama had pinned on my shirt pocket. It said in capital letters underlined twice: LEARN THIS BY MEMORY. When Mama wanted me to do something, she underlined it. The paper said: *My name is Jesús Lendián Gómez*, as if I didn't even know my name, and *I'm eight years old*, which wasn't true because I was nearly nine. Then she had written what I had to learn by heart: *My grandfather is Francisco Lendián. He lives at 243 Michigan Avenue, Miami Beach, and his telephone number is 532-3054.*

Clipped to the slip were my passport and a "visa waiver." Visa waivers were very hard to get in Cuba. Papa and Mama spent over a year trying to get one for my brother and me. Tony promised he'd kill me if I lost it, so I held it tight, closed my eyes, and kept repeating "Francisco Lendián, 243 Michigan Avenue, 532-3054."

I was just beginning to say this a fourth time when the blonde lady talking on the intercom announced that "in case of a loss of pressure in the cabin, masks like these will drop in front of you."

She took a mask that looked just like the one they used on me for my tonsil operation, and slipped it over her face. She told us to put out our cigarettes and to breathe normally.

Then, she said, "In case of an emergency you'll find a life jacket under your seat." She put hers on and told us not to inflate ours till we were outside the plane.

"What happens if we inflate them inside the plane?" I asked Tony.

"You won't get through the door idiot. Can't you see how narrow they are?"

"So you get stuck; then what happens?"

My brother crossed his eyes and stuck out his tongue.

The engines roared and the plane moved up the runway. I pressed my nose against the window to see if I could spot Papa or Mama, but all I saw was a bunch of people waving handkerchiefs. I put my own handkerchief up to the glass and waved good-bye. I'm sure Mama couldn't see me. The plane was zooming up the runway. My stomach climbed and something pulled me to the seat.

As soon as the plane took off I began seeing Havana from above. It looked like a city of elves: the cars like little toys; the royal palm trees, always so tall from the ground up, now looked like small paintbrushes. All of a sudden we could barely see anything. We were crossing a cloud. Clouds are like smoke; there is no falling on them, only through them, till you smash.

The next clouds were dark and looked like mountains. The airplane took a bump and dropped. I was scared, but I didn't tell my brother. Instead, I kept swallowing, hoping I could swallow the knot in my throat. I pretended to be looking out the cabin window so my brother wouldn't catch me crying.

Now I *have* to go to the bathroom, I thought. And the bathroom was way in the back. Every time someone went in, a light turned on. I got up to go, but my brother stuck out his foot and tripped me. I grabbed a man's leg across the aisle. Otherwise, I would have fallen flat on my face. It seemed like everybody else was in a hurry to go, too, because there was a line. One of the men noticed the look on my face and let me go first.

The bathroom was the smallest I'd ever seen. When you pushed on the toilet handle—not really a handle but a pedal—it made a big swoosh and the bottom opened up. Did it all go out into the clouds? The soap, which smelled like something you'd use to wash your dog, squirted through a pipe. The toilet paper was slippery. Maybe that's why there were scented paper towels.

When I tried to get out, the door jammed. I

banged on it till somebody opened it for me. I didn't want to travel all the way to Miami locked up in the bathroom. On my way back I noticed the pilot and co-pilot's cabin door open. I almost slipped in to see the cockpit, but the blonde lady asked me if I wanted something. "Water," I said. She gave me a paper cup filled with ice. I love to chew on ice. They wouldn't let me at home. It gives you cavities.

The flight attendant was passing out candy. There was no candy in Cuba anymore, so I took all I could.

Then I opened my tote bag. It looked like a suitcase, but it wasn't. It was longer and it was made of thick cloth. Mama had put wheels on mine so I could pull it. Inside, she had packed a checkered flannel sport coat for me. Mama had made it out of my grandmother's shawl, and it smelled funny—like mothballs.

Mama also had packed about twenty pairs of socks. They had cost her five pounds of coffee and five pounds of black beans. Mama was an expert in trading. She could make chickenless chicken salad with a yummy carrot sauce, instead of mayonnaise, which she traded for sheets or towels, or the bottom half of old Coke bottles, that we used as glasses.

Papa had invented a brake fluid he made with

castor oil. He was always looking around for screws and wires and things. He came up with weird stuff sometimes, like my brother's shoes, for instance. They were canary yellow with air holes, and had belonged to a Russian. He had traded them for a bottle of pure alcohol that Papa had gotten from a friend for some eggs. Papa raised chickens, so he could use eggs instead of money. Money is no good when you can't get food. You can't eat a peso or even a dollar.

Stuffed in my tote bag I also found a bunch of shorts that Grandma had made from old sheets, a picture of Mama and Papa, and a box of pills. Grandma had told me to take the round ones if I couldn't go to the bathroom, the red ones if I had diarrhea, and the yellow pills if I had a fever. The green cough syrup was for if I caught cold. I guess she thought she wouldn't be around to nurse me the next time I got sick.

Then I found something I was sure Tata, my black nanny, had put in: a piece of black jet to cast off the evil eye. Papa thought that was superstition, but she insisted. A niece of hers was once given the evil eye and shrank till she looked like a monkey.

Tata loved me a lot. She had taken care of me since I was born. She said I was really her child. She made the best candy, even when there was no sugar. When we'd left for the airport, she had held on to the car window crying "My child, my child," till the car sped up and left her behind.

Now I thought I might never see her again. "Suppose Grandfather Franciso Lendián isn't at the Miami airport waiting for us?" I asked Tony.

"We'll call him up."

"Suppose he doesn't answer?"

"We'll get a policeman to help us."

I wasn't going to call a policeman. I had stopped believing in cops the day one of them, in a long beard and an olive-colored uniform, took Papa away at gunpoint. We'd spent days without seeing him, or knowing where he was. One day, Yayo, the gardener, came to our house and told Mama that Papa had been taken to a parochial school, the same one I had gone to before the communists took it over.

As soon as I heard, I slipped out and ran all the way to an old mango tree that stood behind the school wall. I climbed the tree and looked into the yard where we used to have recess. I saw about two hundred men walking in circles. I whistled like the Lendiáns do: a whistle invented by my grandfather that can be heard two miles away. Papa looked up.

"What are you doing here, Kiki?" he asked, coming close to the wall. "Go away before they see you! This is no school now; it's a jail!"

I asked him if he had seen Father Joselín, the priest who played soccer with us.

"He's gone. They all left yesterday. Now go. Tell your mother I'm OK and to send me food."

It wasn't true; not all the priests had left. Some were in jail. However, the day after, Candita, our next-door neighbor, told Mama that one of my teachers had been shot. He had cried "Long live Christ the King!" and "Long live free Cuba!" before the firing squad. Then they shot him. In my mind, I saw him grabbing his stomach and spitting blood.

I tried not to think about it because if I did, I'd dream. If I dreamed, I'd get nightmares. I'm afraid of nightmares; Tata says they come true.

Mama had told us that she and Papa were staying behind so the government wouldn't take away our house and our farm. That's what they did to everybody who left Cuba. Tony and I and my cousins were going to a big school in Miami. She said it had baseball fields, tennis courts, swimming pools, and even horses!

Then she kissed us good-bye and held back her tears. "Send me a snapshot with your horse," she said, trying to smile. Papa hugged me and told me to behave like a man. Grandmother's nose turned tomato-red. She kept sighing, "Oh, Lord! Sacred heart of Jesus!" while she held her rosary in her hands.

I didn't want to leave the waiting room, even if it meant never going to that big school or having a horse. But my brother had pushed me into the fishbowl: a cold air-conditioned waiting room surrounded by glass panels on all sides. Once you went into the fishbowl, you could see your family, but you couldn't talk to them or touch them. As I went in, I noticed a man with his hands pressed hard against the glass. His wife stood on the other side. Both of them were crying. I'd never seen a man crying like that. Then a militia woman told us to go into Customs and strip.

I didn't want to take my clothes off because I didn't want anyone to see my shorts made from worn-out sheets. A thin, bossy militia man with a submachine gun in his hand ordered us, "Get in there and strip!"

That's when I realized all this business about school and horses was a lot of baloney. Nobody has to strip to go to school abroad. As I stood there naked I saw my cousins. I'd never seen all four boys naked, but no one protested. They searched us, then ordered us to dress. When I felt my pockets I found they had taken the watch Papa gave me in advance for my ninth birthday.

They'd also stolen our religious medals. When

my cousins complained, the militia man called them "worms." Being a "worm" in Cuba is terrible; it means you are against the revolution. People were sent to the firing squad just for being "worms."

I thought that if all this stuff about school was baloney, the story about Grandpa Lendián being there to meet us might not be true either.

"Tony, suppose Grandpa isn't in Miami to meet us?"

"Don't be a pest, Kiki. Of course he'll be there; Mama talked to him on the phone. Now sit still and practice your English!"

Nervously, I kept repeating what I'd been taught: "I-dunno, I-dunno, I-dunno," which means "I don't know." That's all I'd have to say to avoid trouble if they asked me anything about Cuba. I also knew how to say "help" and "food," in case I got hungry. My brother had also taught me two bad words: "hell" and "damn."

If Grandpa didn't meet us at the airport, at least we were all together, my brother and I, my four boy cousins and a fifth cousin, María.

My oldest cousin was Manuel (we called him Manolo). Back in Cuba he was always lifting weights to be strong. He had a motorcycle he didn't let me ride. But he got his punishment for being so selfish: he crashed and could never get the spare parts to fix the damage.

María was thirteen. She pretended she was older, though. She already wore a bra and lipstick, even though her family didn't let her. She spent all day listening to music and thinking about her boyfriend. He had been drafted into the revolutionary army and could not leave Cuba till he was thirty. But he would never get to come. They sent him to Angola and he died there.

Cousin Cleto also came along. Cleto was short for Anacleto, a weird name for a boy. He wore braces on his teeth. I wanted braces too, but the dentist said I didn't need them.

Jorge was my favorite cousin; he always did what I said because I was older. Then there was my youngest cousin, Pancho. Poor guy, he always wanted to play with us, but we wouldn't let him. Now he was crying for his mom. Back home he was kind of nutty. Sometimes he would pretend to be a car, then at others he would spread his wings and go "brrrr" like an airplane. Also, he would have these chats with an invisible friend, sometimes changing voices and being the other guy.

My cousins weren't supposed to go with Grandfather Lendián. They were going to a big school called Matecumbe. Later I found out that Matecumbe was really a place where they sent Cuban kids who arrived without their parents.

Now, they were saying something I couldn't understand. The blonde lady sprayed us with something that smelled like Grandma's bug killer. The plane began to shake. I looked out the window.

"Look, Tony! Miami! Down there!"

My ears hurt. I could hardly hear Tony when he said, "Swallow!"

I kept swallowing and listening to the loud-speaker say in Spanish that we were landing. They told us to stay in our seats until the plane had stopped.

"Bienvenidos a Miami, señores pasajeros. Favor de permanecer en sus asientos hasta que el avión..."

But I ignored the instructions and grabbed my tote bag to get out of the plane first. My cousins came scrambling from behind to catch up with me and Tony. At the ladder, Tony said good-bye to the blonde lady and thanked her. He was just pretending to be polite. Then he took my hand. I hated that, so I shook myself free.

"Kiki, remember what Papa said."

"All Papa said was I should behave!"

II

Grandpa and the Ghost

It was hot outside, same as in Cuba. Grandma
had made me put on a wool suit, so I'd have it if it
got cold. But it wasn't cold and I was itchy. If old
folks feel the cold so much, I wonder why they
don't wrap themselves instead of us.

We walked a long way from the plane before we
finally entered the airport building through a glass
door. It opened by itself when we stepped on the
mat before it. To find out how it worked I turned
around to walk in again. Again it opened, like
magic. This was my first American puzzle.

Inside the airport building my ears cleared; the
noise came rushing in. They took us to the
Immigration Desk. The man there looked at me
grimly. He took my visa, stamped it from an ink
pad and handed it to my brother. They asked him
lots of questions about Cuba, but not me. I didn't
even get a chance to say *I-dunno*.

We had just left the Immigration Desk when my
cousins found Tito, a Cuban who worked as a vol-
unteer meeting children at the airport. He was

wearing short pants, a plaid shirt, long socks, tennis shoes, and a funny hat with a red feather. He
was bowlegged and looked ridiculous. Where was
the costume party, I wondered. But he wasn't the
only one. Everybody else seemed to be dressed in
bright colors: men with green or red jackets, and
little hats; women with big flowery dresses. So different from Cuba! In Cuba it was hard to get
clothes anyway. Suddenly, twenty kids crowded
around Tito. He asked their names, checked each
against his list and gave them chewing gum. I
asked if he could give me some and he did.

Then he asked my cousins if they had a place to
stay. Since people in Cuba heard Castro was going
to ship their children to Russia, many kids had
arrived and there wasn't enough room for them all.
My cousins assured him they could stay at
Grandpa's. He left with the other kids, and we all
sat down to wait. We must have waited two hours.
To pass the time I watched all the arriving planes.
The sky turned dark and I felt hungry and afraid.
There were a lot of people there, but nobody
noticed us. Nobody cared.

"Here he comes!" my brother said.

Walking toward us I saw the same old man
whose picture hung in our living room at home,
only now he was older and balder. He recognized
Tony right away and asked him when we had

arrived. His mustache stung when he kissed me. Up to that point he seemed okay, but as soon as our cousins told him they were coming along also, he protested:

"I can't take care of so many kids! I'm an old man! Besides, where will I put you? I haven't even received the money my son said he'd send me! How can I buy food for seven kids?"

My cousin María began to cry. Grandpa said he wasn't running a hotel, and he kept repeating over and over: "Seven kids! Seven kids! Oh, God! Seven kids!"

He called someone from a public telephone and, as he talked, he kept putting his hands on his bald head. He went up to a cop and explained his problem. Finally, since my cousin was crying even harder, he gave in.

"All right, all right, you all come with me today, but first thing tomorrow I'll clear up this mess. Can you imagine?" he said to himself out loud. "They've got to be joking! Who ever thought of sending seven kids to an old man? Come on, let's go, let's go, let's go!"

He herded us into an old Cadillac and off we went. The back seat had a big hole and all the stuffing was coming out. There was another hole in the floor; I could see the street speeding underneath.

"Look, Grandpa, if I stick my foot through the hole I can touch the street," I said.

"Well don't and stop complaining. This is just something to get around in. I got it for three hundred dollars: that's all we exiles can afford when we get here.

"Don't worry Grandpa. It's great. This way you don't need air conditioning."

I looked through the window. Miami looked like a lit Christmas tree. We went over a very long bridge that was really a road with water on both sides. I saw all kinds of boats and a lot of people fishing. I also saw canals with big houses at the water's edge. I asked Grandpa if one of them was his.

"Are you kidding, boy? The only thing we exiles have is a ten-pound bag of hunger."

I didn't know what an exile was, but noticing so many folks on the street looking old and miserable, I took them to be exiles, whatever that meant. Neither did I know what Grandpa meant by a ten-pound bag of hunger. I sure learned later.

I asked Grandpa if there were sharks in Miami and if it was true that in the aquarium they had a man who rode on dolphins' backs and played ball with them. And where were the alligators? When could he take me to the beach or fishing in a boat?

"Yes, yes. You'll go to the beach. It's free. But

now let's see how long you can keep quiet, uh?"

After what seemed like a thousand turns, he drove up a broad avenue that twisted into a narrow lane till we reached a shabby wooden house. Everything was dark, like in mystery movies.

"Is this Michigan?" I asked.

"No, this is not Michigan!" he answered crossly.

I hadn't said it to bother him; I was just remembering the paper with his address.

"Michigan is the name of the hotel I stayed at when I arrived. My nephew José rented this house before he went to New York to get a job. He said I might as well live here and save some money."

"Oh."

"He's certainly not a millionaire," my brother observed.

The more lights Grandpa turned on, the older and shabbier the house looked.

"OK, this is all I've got. Just four beds. You'll have to make it do. Good night."

"But Grandpa, we haven't eaten!" Tony complained.

"The kitchen's in the back. José left bread and hot dogs in the ice box, also some milk. Eat what you want. We'll think of something for tomorrow."

But the next day he didn't.

Again for breakfast we had hot dogs, bread, and powdered milk. And again that night and the next day, till there was almost nothing left. Tony and Manolo worried that Grandpa was going to starve us to death, but I didn't think so. It's just that old folks hardly eat anything because nothing agrees with them.

Grandpa seemed very old, like a thousand years maybe. The top of his head was smooth and shiny, as if it had never had a hair on it. It took him a long time to sit down or stand up. At night he took out his teeth and put them in a glass. He was always forgetting everything, and getting himself all mixed up. He called Tony, Manolo; and me, Cleto. Sometimes he couldn't come up with any name at all and he'd say: "Hey, you boy! Now, what's your name?" Also, he'd start saying one thing and end up saying something else. I think he didn't say what he wanted to, but what he could.

Sometimes Grandpa would just stare at the back of his hands or shake his head yes and no, though there was nobody there asking him anything. He smelled like *Vick's Vaporub* and a little like a hospital room. You'd have to tell him things twice for them to sink in. He couldn't hear you if you didn't shout, but if you shouted too loud, his ears rang. Sometimes I'd sit by his side and he'd tell me all about his aches, or nearly all. When it rained, even his fingernails hurt. At other times, he'd tell me the same old stories, like way back in Cuba when he

used to plant potatoes and he owned a lot of farms
and had been president of this or that club. But the
one he enjoyed the most—it made him laugh and
slap his knee—was the story of the time he was a
baseball player. Grandpa had been a pitcher!

Grandpa had us eating hot dogs not because he
was mean, but because he didn't remember. When
I told him there was hardly anything left to eat, he
answered, "Adela will think of something."

I was relieved until Tony told me that Adela was
our grandmother, who had died when Papa was a
child.

"Tony, is something wrong with Grandpa?"

"Plenty. He is old and he forgets things."

"You mean he'll forget to buy food? I'm hungry!"

"We still have a few hot dogs."

"I'm sick of hot dogs!"

"Then go hungry. That's all there is."

Four days had passed and we didn't go anywhere. We were bored stiff, so we'd sit and watch
TV for hours. Grandfather couldn't stand noise and
he hated TV anyway. So when it broke and we
asked if someone could repair it he said:

"No, no. We don't need it. You sit there like
dummies and you don't get any exercise! Find
something better to do."

Tony did. He found an old set of drums and

started practicing. He practiced so much Grandpa was ready to climb the walls. Once in a while, he would pop out of his room and yell, "For God's sake, stop that racket!"

Soon we found better things to do. Cleto didn't really mean to break the iron and the toaster. Nor the fan, either. He just wanted to find out how things work. Maybe he put some screws in the wrong place, because they never worked again. Manolo wanted to practice his judo, so he put the mattresses on the floor. Jorge and I thought it would be fun to explore space. We built a rocket with the trash can and some boxes. We set it up in a tree and were ready to launch it with Panchito as pilot when Grandpa had a fit.

"Take that kid out of that contraption! He'll get hurt! We have no insurance!"

Grandpa was so upset he had to sit down, his face got red and he fanned himself as if he couldn't breathe.

"This is too much! Too much!" he gasped. "I'm too old for this!"

Then he stood up, waved his finger at us and used the old Cuban formula for scolding:

"*¡Dios los va a castigar!* God is going to punish you!"

Sure enough, that night, when I was going to bed I looked out of the window and I saw a ghost. It

was all in black; it held a candle in one hand and a
skull in the other.

I began to scream.

"Tony, Manolo! There's a ghost at the window!
Hurry!"

When they looked, it was gone.

That night I couldn't sleep. There was a towel
hanging from a clothes hanger, and it looked like a
hanged man. The branches scraped against the window, like ghosts trying to get in.

"Tony?"

"What?"

"Do you think God is trying to punish me?"

"No, Kiki, I don't think so."

"Then why did I see that ghost in the window?"

"Because you're scared and you imagine things. That's why."

"I saw it. I swear I saw it."

"OK, go to sleep now."

"Tony?"

"Now what?"

"Once I saw a lady talking to Mama. She was a Jehovah's fitness. She said the world would come to an end because people were behaving so badly."

"Jehovah's Witness, Kiki."

"That's it."

"Now knock it off and go to sleep!"

Next day, Tony was out in the yard, when he cried, "Manolo, come quick! Hurry!"

"What's wrong?"

"I just saw the ghost!"

"Come on, Tony, you, too?"

"No, I swear. It ran across the yard and hid behind the bushes. Come!"

"What are you going to do?" Manolo was scared.

"Catch him! You head right; I'll head left!"

They started walking toward the fence very slowly. Silently, they went around it.

"There!" Tony cried. The ghost was bundled up against the other side of the fence.

Tony jumped, grabbed it, but it started to fight to get away.

Manolo used one of his judo locks to immobilize it.

"Hey! What's this? What are you doing?" it cried.

By now Tony had pulled off his mask.

"*¡Es el americano!* It's the American!" he cried in surprise.

"The guy next door!" cried Manolo.

"You came to our house last night," Tony said menacingly and tightened his grip on him.

"So?"

"So you scared my little brother."

"Yes, I thought I would!"

"You mean you wanted to frighten him?"

"Sure. It's Halloween!"

But neither Tony nor Manolo knew what Halloween meant. So Tony punched him in the stomach and said, "Just so you remember not to frighten my brother again!"

The ex-ghost said, "Ouch!" and bent over.

Then, as Tony and Manolo walked away, he shouted:

"You Cubans! You're crazy! Why can't you have some fun?"

III

Our First Supermarket

By now we were pretty desperate. For five days we had eaten nothing but hot dogs and powdered milk. We were all getting thin and pale.

Poor cousin Panchito begged for food all day long. Every time he heard a plane, he'd run outside, raise his arms and call for his mother and father as if they were up there and could hear him. He had turned so skinny you could almost see through him. He no longer pretended to be a car and he hardly ever talked to himself anymore.

Cousin María would try to comfort him by offering him powdered milk with sugar.

But he refused to eat or drink.

"I want fried plantains!" he cried. "Rice and eggs and fried plantains!"

"I would like *arroz con pollo!*" cried Cleto.

Even Tony looked thoughtful and said, "I think I could eat ten *paellas.*"

"Quit talking nonsense, and let's do something about it!" cried Manolo.

"Like what?"

"Like talk to Grandpa."

"OK, let's go."

When he saw the seven of us marching into his room, Grandpa sat up in bed, put his hands to his head and said, "Oh God! What now?"

Tony took the lead.

"We cannot go on this way."

"You can't go on this way! What about me?"

"I know it's been hard on you, but we're starved."

Grandpa put his hands in his pocket, took out a five dollar bill and waved it at us.

"See this? It's all I have left. And the rent is due this week."

"Then, Manolo and I will have to find some work, Grandpa," Tony said.

"Sure, you could mow lawns or wash cars. Only just try in this neighborhood! No one has a penny. They're practically all refugees, the same as you and me. And it's not easy to get a decent job. Especially if you don't speak English."

"So what do Cubans do for a living?"

"I'll tell you what they do for a living! María Portela raffles off the good linen she brought from Cuba. Modesto picks tomatoes. He was a lawyer in Cuba, mind you. Rafael decided to start his own business as a barber."

At the thought of Rafael, Grandpa slapped his

knee and started laughing.

"You could fill a book with all the stories! One day a lady walked in with her boy to get the boy's hair cut; Rafael took this electric razor which he didn't quite know how to use. The thing went off by itself and the boy ended with a bald strip running all the way from his nape to his forehead."

"OK, Grandpa, but there must be something we can do," protested Manolo.

"Yes. Go to Coral Gables. There are plenty of rich people there."

"Where is it?"

"Thirty miles from here."

"Would you lend me your car?" Tony asked.

"Drive without a license and no insurance? You'll land in jail!"

"We can't go on like this! I won't let Panchito starve!" María cried, her eyes filled with tears.

"There, there, girl. Take the five dollars; go buy some food. Tomorrow we'll think of something. I've already talked to two priests and three reverends. They'll help us."

"OK kids, let's go shopping!" María said, and we all marched out of the house.

We didn't know where the grocery store was, and none of us knew enough English to ask, so we followed María into what was a drugstore but didn't look like one. Drugstores in Cuba sold only medicine, but here in the United States they also sell toys, electric fans, radios and even stoves.

There was a soda fountain in the back.

"Look, Tony!" I pointed to a photograph of a chocolate ice cream cup with a cherry on top.

Tony figured out each ice cream was a dollar: too much!

"We can't afford it, Kiki!"

"Food," I said to the cashier. He must have understood me because he pointed to a supermarket sign about two blocks away.

The name of the supermarket was Food Fair. My parents used to talk about all the things you could buy in Cuba before the revolution, but I had never seen so much food in one place: shelves and more shelves of cans and loaves of bread, shelves loaded with vegetables and fruit, and a very long kind of stand, with ice on the inside, full of fish and chickens and meat.

We couldn't believe our eyes.

"Look, Tony! Ham!"

"Cake!" said Cleto.

"Look! Pears and apples!" said Tony. "I haven't seen them in years!"

"Pizzas! All kinds of pizzas! Real pizzas! Mozzarella, pepperoni, cheese!"

Before we knew it, we were each grabbing things and putting them in the cart.

"Stop! Stop!" María cried. She started putting everything back on the shelves. "We have five dollars. Understand? Five dollars. We can't go crazy! Look at the price tags. Get what's cheapest."

"Everything marked special is cheaper," observed Manolo.

"All right, you bring the specials."

"Yesterday's doughnuts are half price," said Cleto, who loved doughnuts.

"OK, take some. But now I'll choose the specials. Tony, you take a note of the prices and start adding."

We were all so busy we completely lost track of Panchito.

Finally, we had a half-empty cart of essentials, and we waited in line in front of the cashier.

Tony placed all the packages on the counter and the lady took them one by one, looked at the tag and rang up the price, while we stood keeping count of everything and adding as fast as we could.

Finally she said, "It's four ninety five."

María and Tony exchanged a smile. "We made it!" María whispered. She took out her wallet, carefully unfolded the five dollar bill and handed it to the cashier.

Just then Panchito came running toward us and started taking things out of his pocket and laying them on the counter.

"Chocolate, cookies, chocolate bars, chewing gum, lollipops, Life Savers!" he announced proudly as he put them down.

"Where did you get all this?"

"From the shelves. They have shelves and shelves of candy!"

María leaned towards him.

"We don't have any money left, Panchito. You must put everything back."

"Nobody said I couldn't take them!" Panchito protested.

"But you can't, Panchito. That's stealing!"

Panchito bit his lip and started picking up the candy as a tear trickled down his cheek.

"No, no! You go ahead and take them. It's a gift from me!"

I looked at the cashier in disbelief and saw her for the first time.

Her name was Esther; she had it written on the lapel of her white uniform. Her hair was dyed red, but her eyebrows and the hair over her lips were black. She had on lots of makeup and her eyelids flickered green every time she blinked. When she smiled, her wrinkles quivered like little caterpillars.

"Cubans?" she asked me.

"Yes, Cubans," I answered.

Suddenly her face clouded and her eyes watered. Then she lifted her sleeve so we could see a number tattooed on her arm.

"Good luck, children," was all she said.

"Why did she lift her sleeve, Tony?" I asked once we were outside.

"Because she's Jewish, I guess."

"Do they put numbers on Jews here?"

"No, they numbered them during the war when they were sent to concentration camps."

"What are concentration camps?"

"You must've seen them a thousand times in the movies. They were places where people were treated terribly and made to work very hard."

"Like in Cuba, huh?"

"Worse. Millions got killed. They were ordered to take showers. Then, instead of water, they got sprayed with gas and died."

"All of them?"

"No, some starved to death."

"Oh, now I know why."

"Why what?"

"Why she let Panchito take all the candy."

"Yeah, I guess."

That night we had a feast. María cooked rice and eggs with plantains. We started talking about our families. It was almost twelve o'clock when María carried Panchito to bed. She was humming a song my mother used to sing to me, and it made me homesick.

IV

Bad News and the Parrots

We were still asleep the next morning when the doorbell rang. Tony opened the door. Standing outside was a man with ugly sunburn blisters covering his hands.

"Does Francisco Lendián live here?" He was Cuban.

"Yes, sir."

"Could I speak to him?"

"He's still asleep."

"Are you his grandson?"

"Yes, sir."

"Tony?"

"Yes, and this is my brother Kiki."

"I have a message for your grandfather from his son."

"You mean my father?"

"Yes, I came on a raft from Cuba two days ago. I didn't leave the hospital till today."

"On a raft? *Caramba!*"

"It was pretty bad, we nearly sank. Twenty of us. We're here thanks to an American Coast Guard ship that picked us up. We had no food or water for two days. But we're here now."

"Everything was OK in Cuba when you left?"

"No, it's terrible. Things get worse by the day."

"What about our parents?"

"They're desperate; they haven't heard from you. Your father doesn't know if your grandfather received the two thousand dollars he sent through a friend in Canada. It's very risky to try to get dollars out of Cuba, you know. If they catch you trying to change pesos for dollars, you end up in jail. Besides, nobody has dollars anymore."

"Grandpa hasn't received any mail."

"Find out. Maybe the money arrived before you did. Your father gave a lady in Cuba ten thousand pesos. Her son, who's in Canada, was supposed to send two thousand dollars to your grandfather."

Tony shrugged. "I don't think he did. Not yet, anyway."

"Ask your grandfather. Your mother's dying to get out of Cuba, even if it's in a rowboat. They are taking dangerous risks. I warned them. The coast is under very strict watch."

We knew what he meant.

"Any boat caught slipping out, it's gunfire first and questions later, if you're still alive. In my case, I had no choice. They wouldn't let me go; they don't allow technicians to leave the country. But your parents can wait and leave legally. Is your grandfather taking care of that?"

"We just don't know."

"Remind him, because I won't be back. I'm leaving for New York to meet my wife and children. Tell him he must send your parents an affidavit and a work contract. They already have visas for Mexico, but if they don't get the paperwork in time, their visas will expire and they'll never be able to come. An affidavit and a work contract, don't forget!"

"We won't."

"Good luck. Sorry we can't shake hands. It's the blisters, see?"

"Tony, what's an affidavit?" I asked when the man left.

"A paper signed by an American, saying he's responsible for Mama and Papa's expenses. Or something like that," he answered.

"And what American is going to sign it for you if we don't know anyone here?"

"I don't know."

This, coming from Tony, who would never let me see he didn't know everything, really worried me.

"So, who's going to give you a work contract?" I insisted.

"That's enough! We'll see."

"If Grandpa can't do it, and you know nothing about getting affidavits, or whatever you call 'em, Papa and Mama will never leave Cuba."

"Why do you always see the dark side of everything, Kiki?"

"Tony?"

"Yeah."

"You think they'll try to get away in a boat?"

"Maybe."

"Tony?"

"Yes?"

"The man said they'd shoot them."

"Yeah."

"What with?"

"Machine guns, I suppose."

"Tony?"

"Will you shut up!"

"I just can't stop thinking. If Mama and Papa try to make it over in a boat and get shot with machine guns, they'll die!"

"They're not coming in a boat!" Tony assured me.

That night I had a nightmare. Papa and Mama were in a small boat, rowing. Mama was screaming because Papa was shot and wounded and fell into the water. She couldn't pull him out and he was drowning.

"Tony! Tony!" I cried.

"Wake up, Kiki! Everything is going to be all right!"

It was good to hear his voice calling me. He sounded like my father.

Everything was all right for a few days. But soon we ran out of food and knew we couldn't ask Grandpa for more money. That's when Cleto, the one with the braces, came up with the idea of taking fruit from our next-door neighbor. She had a yard full of mango trees, bananas, avocados, and oranges. She also raised parrots. Luckily, the neighbor was a widow living all alone.

We decided that Tony and Manolo would jump the fence, while the rest of us kept an eye on the old lady. The plan worked fine for a few days until Manolo complained he had his fill of fruit and would rather switch to roasted parrots.

We couldn't catch any. They raised such a squawk that the lady came out and Manolo had to hide. But she saw him, and came right to our house to complain. She was angry and upset. María answered the door politely and asked the lady to sit down. As soon as she heard María speak Spanish, the lady looked thrilled.

"Ah, but you're Cubans! How wonderful! I'm Cuban, too."

"Cuban?" María wondered. The lady spoke Spanish with a funny accent and she couldn't roll her Rs.

"Well, I mean to say I feel Cuban. I was born in Russia, but I really don't remember anything about it because I left very young. My sister and I escaped to Poland with our parents. It was terrible. As young girls we had to dress in black, like old ladies, for fear of the soldiers. We fled again when the German army invaded Poland. Guess how I escaped? Tied underneath a cart.

"I got help from other Jewish families," she continued, "I made it to Paris and finally to Cuba. My husband had a store in Old Havana, on Muralla Street. The Cubans treated us very well. That's why I love Cuba so much. After the revolution we decided to leave. We knew it would end up in communism, as in Poland. But Simon, my husband, died and now I'm alone.

"I've been through so much! If it weren't for my little parrots..."

The old lady sighed. María took the chance to put in: "We've also been through a lot. Right now—can you imagine—we have nothing to eat."

"Nothing?"

"No, *señora*, nothing at all. That's why my cousin took fruit from your yard."

"Why, that's awful, just awful! I'll go home right now and fix you a nice hot meal."

An hour later she returned with a pile of pots stacked together. She placed them on the kitchen table, taking the lids off one by one.

"Look, children! Roast beef, fried plantains, black beans, rice..."

We didn't give her time to finish. Before she knew it, everything was gone.

"How awful! Poor kids!" The lady put on a sad face. "Just like wolves."

V

Foster Home

To this day, Tony believes the old lady was the one who called Child Welfare. The very next day we heard a car stop in front of the house. Through the blinds we saw a lady with a briefcase. She was tall and stiff, wore dark glasses and had the face of a school principal. We were afraid to open the front door, so she slipped in through the back. Before we knew it, she was in the middle of the living room asking questions.

"Who's the oldest one here?"

Both Manolo and Tony said they were. She wrote down everybody's name and age.

"Is there an adult here to look after you?"

"My grandfather," I said.

"He's ill?"

"He forgets things. And maybe he had a heart attack."

"Hasn't left his room in a week," added Tony.

"We haven't got a thing to eat," said María.

"Oh, this is terrible, terrible!" the lady said over and over. "I'll report this right away and return tomorrow."

Next day, when she came back, she called us.

"Let's see: Manuel, Jorge and Anacleto Gómez."

"That's us," said my cousins.

"Antonio and Jesús Lendián."

"That's us," answered my brother.

"Good. You're going to a foster home."

Before I had time to ask what that was, the lady turned to María.

"You're lucky, I've found you a scholarship to a wonderful school. It's run by nuns."

"What about my little brother?"

"We'll have to send him to..."

María didn't let the lady finish. She picked up Panchito in her arms, hugged him, and shouted furiously. "You'll have to kill me before you take my brother away from me!"

"Look, child, this is as sad for me as it is for you. But do you realize how hard it is to find a place for seven children? Every day we get more than we can care for. We can't cope."

"Why don't you just leave us here and let us have some food? We're cousins, we don't want to be split up."

"Let me see what we can do for you, María. The rest of you, pack your clothes. I'll be back for you tomorrow at eight."

The lady returned the next day. She brought a

policeman. Both of them sat in the living room and she said:

"I can't leave you here. By law, all children in this country must go to school. For you, María, I've found a Cuban family who's willing to take you and your little brother in. You'll feel at home with them. The rest of you must go where we send you."

"But suppose we don't want to?" Tony demanded.

"In that case, we'll have to take you to court and let the judge decide. And that could be worse; the court might send you to Colorado or some northern state. Chances are you would never see your brother again."

Tony moved to sit next to María. He whispered:

"Look, it's better for you to go your way with Panchito. Let's not look for more trouble."

"And what about our grandfather?" I asked the lady.

"He'll be taken to a hospital."

By now the policeman had become impatient.

"O.K., let's go, let's go!" he ordered.

First, we left María and Panchito at a little green house where the people came out to greet us in Spanish. We said good-bye quietly. My last hope, as I watched María and Panchito move away hand in hand, was that they'd get enough to eat.

"*Adios*, María, I'll call you when I can," Tony promised sadly.

Later we left our cousins at Matecumbe.

"*Hasta luego,* cousins," Tony and I said.

"See you soon," Manolo returned.

We all knew soon might be never, but we pretended otherwise.

Cleto bit his lip and said good-bye.

✳   ✳   ✳

I wondered where they were taking Tony and me. Way out of town, it seemed. We drove on an expressway that crossed over others, till we came to one they called the Palmetto, and then to another road they called Tamiami. On one side there was a canal lined with tall pines, like those that used to grow near the beach in Havana. We kept on traveling and soon we left Miami behind us. The land was flat, crisscrossed by canals and full of small trees and tall sawgrass. If you looked closely, there was water or mud everywhere.

Finally we got to a place that looked like a restaurant. Outside there was a large pink plaster flamingo standing on one foot and a fake alligator with its mouth wide open. A sign hung from its snout saying "Alligator Hamburgers." Just the thought of alligator meat made me sick.

Behind the restaurant there was an old wooden house, and around it, a junkyard full of old trucks, broken bikes and rusty cars without tires, steering wheels or fenders. There were several snakes in a wire cage. I also saw an alligator and some turtles. There was a high cage with a little tiger, only it wasn't a tiger but a big cat that wasn't a cat, either.

What I liked most about the place was that behind the house there was a canal and some flat boats with motors that made lots of noise. You could hardly see the water; tall grass was growing everywhere.

The first person I saw was a real live Indian girl in a skirt striped with ribbons of different colors. Her hair was braided flat on top of her head. On a bridge nearby there were several black people in straw hats. They were fishing, and it flashed through my mind that some day, if I stayed, I could fish with them, too. Truth is that the place—if it weren't for the mosquitoes that were beginning to bite—looked to me like a lot of fun.

A red headed man, big and fat, met us. That was Mike Jones. He was in a grimy undershirt, patching an old tire. He smelled awful. Using his finger like a wiper he rubbed the sweat off his forehead and stretched out his hand to the lady with us. Then he turned his head and shouted, "Mama, Mama!"

Mama was Mike's wife. She came out to meet us. She looked like a tent in her flowery dress. You could see her grimy toes through the sandals. The couple chuckled, as if happy to see us. I wondered why, since they didn't know us. I looked at them again. His teeth were yellow. The flesh on her face was smooth and puffy like a blown-up balloon.

They immediately turned to talk to the lady from the child welfare agency. They said yes to what I supposed were instructions or a description of who we were. I still don't know, because at the time we couldn't understand one word of English.

"Juan! Joshua!" the couple shouted.

From inside the house came a very thin, dark-eyed boy who was later to become my best friend, along with another boy who wore a cowboy hat. His hair was down to his shoulders and so blonde, it looked nearly white.

The lady from the agency said good-bye to us and left. We entered the old house. It smelled moldy and damp. There were two covered sofas and still another one with holes in it, a very big television set, a dirty recliner, and several broken chairs. Everything was so filthy that I was glad when Juanito said in Spanish.

"Come along, it's not here but back there."

Back there turned out to be a trailer; inside there

were two bunk beds. Mama put my tote bag on the top one.

The only words she knew in Spanish were *sombrero* and *olé*. She would say them all the time and then double up with laughter. Everything made her laugh and she kept on laughing even when there was nothing to laugh about.

After a while, she said, "Bye-bye, friends." As she left she raised her arms like a Spanish dancer and said, "*olé,*" which came out like *oh-lay*.

I asked the boy, "Does Mama have a loose screw?" and I tipped a finger to my temple.

"No, she wants you to like her. She's nice."

He told me his name was Juan Martínez and that he was a Puerto Rican. I introduced myself as Jesús Lendián.

"Jesús?"

"Yes, Jesús."

"*Ay, bendito!*" he said, and burst out laughing. "Here in the United States you can't go by the name of Jesus. It will only bring you trouble! Why don't you change it right now?"

"Because it's my name and I like it. What's it to you?"

"*Ay bendito,* don't get mad! I didn't mean any harm. Are you an orphan, too?"

"No, my parents live in Cuba."

"Oh, I see." He stared at the floor.

I felt sorry for him, so I said: "Well, I'm almost like an orphan. I never see my parents. They're not here and who knows if I'll ever see them again."

It was his turn to be friendly. He told me that Mama and Mike were good and would treat us nicely, except on Saturdays.

"Why not Saturdays?"

"That's the day they drink a lot of beer and Mike gets mean. It's better to get lost on Saturdays!"

I asked Juan about the airplane boats. He said they were for traveling over the sawgrass. Mike rented them out.

I also asked Juan about the snakes in the cage, and he said they were for the tourists to see, and I had to be careful because they were very dangerous.

"If a coral snake bites you, you'll die in four minutes. There are others that look a lot like coral snakes but they're harmless. They have a black stripe between each red and yellow stripe. The coral snakes have the red and yellow stripes together. No black stripe, understand? Learn the difference; all you have to do is look at the stripes."

I told Juan I'd try, but the only thing I was sure I'd do, if I saw a snake, was run. Juanito said there were big cats running wild and also boars, deer and

bears. I thought he was making up stories to scare
me.

When I asked him how long he had been living
with Mike and Mama, Juanito couldn't remember,
it had been so long. His mother had died in New
York and his father must have died, too, but he
wasn't sure. He had never known him. I felt sorry
for Juanito, but he didn't seem to mind at all.
Maybe he was used to it; he smiled and sang all
day.

"Listen, Juanito, what's this thing they call a foster home?"

"It's a place where the government pays people
to take care of children who have nowhere to go.
There are four of us here now, so Mike and Mama
will become rich!"

So we were a business, I thought, like a restaurant, or fixing cars, or the tourists who came to ride
on a boat over the sawgrass and eat alligator hamburgers.

"Are they really made of alligator meat?"

"What?"

"The hamburgers."

"Have you seen cows around here? Of course,
they're alligator meat!"

From then on Juan and I were buddies.

Osceola, the Indian, also became my friend.
Mike would pay him two dollars to fight the big

alligator each time a bus load of tourists showed up. It was really an old alligator, but the tourists didn't know that. Osceola would fake a struggle with the poor animal. He would force its mouth open, turn him upside down and sit on him. This got the old gator mad and he'd lash back angrily with his tail.

Mike would announce the alligator show. He'd always tell a bunch of lies. The best was the one about the alligator that had killed and eaten two men, and that only the great Osceola dared to wrestle it. The tourists swallowed the story whole and clapped.

When they finally left the poor old alligator

alone, Mike took the visitors for a tour of the
Everglades in his swamp boats with the large airplane propellers. He talked about the wild Indians
that still lived around there, and how thirty years
before they had attacked and burned down a rich
man's home. Later, he invited the tourists to taste
the awful alligator burgers cooked by Mama and to
drink beer. The visitors liked everything and had
their pictures taken with Osceola and the tired alligator.

Sometimes we went fishing, especially on
Sundays, when people from Miami came out to
spend the day. Usually they brought a lot of kids
along and we played with them. At lunchtime, their
mother or grandmother would invite us to share
their fried chicken.

One day, as we were fishing, Juanito said,
"Watch out! See that alligator in the water?"

"Yeah, and also a whale and two sharks," I said.

"Look!" He pointed.

Two beady black eyes were peering at us just
above the water.

Juanito took a stone from the road and threw it
at the eyes. The alligator opened its mouth, slapped
the water with its tail, and disappeared.

When we got home Juanito told Mike about the
alligator, and I said we had eaten fried chicken
with a black family. Mike looked at me though he

couldn't understand my bad English. As he gradually understood he got mad and shouted, "Keep
away from strangers! You hear me?"

Why, I thought. I like strangers. In Cuba my
father and mother taught me to be nice to strangers,
unless they were carrying machine guns. I didn't
say anything because Mike was upset and I was
afraid of him, but I made up my mind to go on
fishing with them and eating their fried chicken
whenever I could.

VI

I Meet a Real Indian Chief

One day Osceola took me to his home in an Indian village. There was a modern building nearby with a sign that read "Miccosukee Tribe Cultural Center," placed so you couldn't miss it from the road. Behind this building, several Indian families lived in worn-out thatched huts that looked like what in Cuba were called *bohios*. A *bohio* had walls, but these Indian huts didn't, just roofs.

There was a totem pole in front of the little shop where Osceola's mother sold things made by the Indians. Only Osceola's family lived there. His parents had a hut and each of his brothers had a separate one like it. All the huts surrounded an empty space. One of them was just a kitchen where a wood fire was always burning.

Osceola's mother was short and moved as if her neck hurt. Her eyebrows were penciled in such a way that they first were straight and then curved upwards. She greeted me very seriously, nodding and speaking in Indian. Later, she began sewing ribbons of many colors on a sewing machine as old as my grandmother's in Cuba.

Osceola's father's name was Homero. He had straight, long hair, his face was very wrinkled and his skin looked like cardboard. I saw him in his hut, carving. He was the one who made the tomahawks, drums and small totems that his wife sold at the store. He didn't say anything, on purpose maybe, so I wouldn't bother him. His eyes were black and small and full of anger. Either he was very tired or sad, or else he didn't want to be my friend. He went on working silently.

On my way out, I offered him my hand. "*Adios, señor.*"

He looked at me for a second and seemed to smile.

There was a sign at the exit: *Admission, fifty cents.*

"That's what we charge the tourists," Osceola explained.

What a pain it must be for the Indians to be at home and have strangers snooping around, paying to see them like monkeys in a zoo, I thought.

"Did my father say anything to you?"

I shook my head.

"Do you wonder why?"

I shrugged.

"You expected to see a big Indian chief with feathers on his head dancing around a fire, huh?"

I said no, but I thought yes.

"We Indians have become distrustful and sad, like my father."

"Does he speak English?"

"Better than I do. He knows a lot of Indian history, too. He's the one who teaches the children here."

"But they go to school, don't they?"

"No, my father doesn't let them."

"Why not?"

"So they won't learn the white man's evil ways and forget their own customs. We send only one or two children to school, so they can read and write in English and look after tribal affairs."

"And the rest learn nothing?"

"On the contrary, they learn a great deal."

"Like what?"

"Like our customs, our crafts, our traditions, our history. They also learn to hunt and fish better than any white kid."

"But isn't there a law here in the United States that all children must go to school?"

"We're not part of the United States," Osceola said, with a hint of pride.

I raised my eyes.

"We're a separate nation," he explained, "and we want to keep it that way."

"So you don't like white people?"

"Some I do, even though most of them haven't treated us right."

Osceola then told me some of the history of his people:

"A long time ago, the Seminole and Miccosukee Indians came south fleeing from the white man. They decided that as long as they could be free they would stay in Florida, where there was hardly anything but swamps. After they had put up their villages and planted their crops, the white man wanted to settle here, too, and began capturing Indians and shipping them west to a territory called Oklahoma. Parents and children were separated and some families were broken up forever. The Indians declared war and for many years fought the white man. One of the Indian leaders was Osceola."

"The same name as yours," I said.

"No, my name is the same as his."

"Chief Osceola fought all his life and was never beaten in battle. Then, the whites sent word that they wanted to sign a peace treaty. They took it to Osceola to sign. But he pulled out his knife and slashed the paper. That was the only signature the white man would ever get from him. Finally, they killed him and his corpse was beheaded.

"The Indians kept on fighting and the United

States kept sending troops. But the Indians could not be defeated. Finally, trying to stop the endless war, the United States government put aside large tracts of land called reservations. The Indians were forced to live there, whether they wanted to or not. A lot of them felt it was like being in prison, so they fled further south into the Everglades.

"But here there was only water, mud, alligators, mosquitoes, and a terrible heat," Osceola said, looking around him. "The Indians died like flies, until only about five hundred were left.

"Much later, since we had no land, we decided to settle by the side of the road, to make some money selling things to tourists. The white man had taken everything from us but still they wouldn't leave us alone."

Osceola probably thought I was not interested in Indian history because he said:

"My great-grandfather was the child of a Spaniard and an Indian mother. His father was a fisherman and took him to Havana to be baptized. That's why my father's name is Homero."

Suddenly he stopped and smiled.

"Kiki, did you know here in the Everglades there are little men, no bigger than your hand, who live underground and come out at night to have fun and do mischief? Also there are serpents that can cast an evil spell just by looking at you."

He went on to tell me that until recently the Indian men wore skirts instead of jeans. They didn't bury their dead in cemeteries either. When his grandfather died, the family took him deep into the swamp, far from the village. They left him in an open hut, made of four thin wooden pillars and a thatched roof. Then, the family brought his shotgun, his pipe and tools and broke them all up, so they would also die and follow the dead chief to the hunting ground where he would go.

Osceola paused a while and added thoughtfully:

"Maybe you don't realize it yet, Kiki, but between us Indians and you Cubans who are coming over, there's something in common, or there should be. Perhaps you can learn from us never to forget your roots. If you do, they may be lost forever."

When I got back to Mike's place, Juanito came out asking a thousand questions: "Did you see the old man? Did he talk to you? When is the corn festival?" But I didn't feel like talking. I was sad.

VII

Paco

In winter the Everglades would fill up with hunters who came in on swamp buggies, trucks with huge fat tires that won't sink in the muck. They brought long shot guns and dogs that pause and smell the air to find the deer.

Once, a Cuban doctor with enough money to spend on guns and bullets invited Juanito and me to go along on a hunt. He taught me how to shoot. He also had some very expensive hunting dogs. Juanito told me they even sent the dogs to special training schools where they were taught to hunt. I thought to myself that the money would be better spent on teaching children and not dogs. But I didn't say anything; I was having a good time and the doctor might not like it.

Early next morning the Cuban doctor roasted a young pig. We all sat around the barbecue pit and sang Cuban songs. It was a lot of fun until later, when the hunters shot a buck and bound his legs around a pole to carry him out of the swamp. The buck's eyes were open, and as they walked he left a trail of dripping blood.

I didn't like the men anymore, even if they were Cubans, like me. I decided that next time, before a hunt, Juanito and I would scare away all the deer. Juanito seemed to be reading my mind. He told me that there was an old lady from Miami who spent all her time fighting against deer hunting in the Everglades. Some people believe it's good to hunt deer to keep their numbers down. But the truth is that most of the hunters kill the animals just for the fun of it.

A lot of motorcycle gangs would also come to the Everglades. The riders wore black helmets, black leather jackets and sunglasses like pilots in old World War II films. You could hardly see their faces. They all wore their hair long and many of the men had beards.

I found Paco thanks to the motorcycles. He was trying to cross the road, but it was dark and the motorcyclists didn't see him, so they ran over him. Juanito and I rescued him. We nursed him and put him in a cage.

Paco was a raccoon. I didn't know how to say raccoon in Spanish because I had never seen one in Cuba. By then I was learning the name for things in English that I had never known in Spanish. And it's been that way ever since. Juanito told me that the word for raccoon in Spanish is *mapache*.

Paco's forelegs looked like little human hands

with fingernails. It was funny to see him hold a nursing bottle. Since Paco was still growing, Osceola told me to set him loose.

"Animals are not toys, Kiki," said Osceola.

He was wrong. Paco was a live toy for me. No one had given me anything to play with in this country, so I made up my mind to keep Paco.

But Osceola insisted that if I really cared for Paco I would turn him loose. Paco clung to my shirt with his sharp nails as if fearing that Osceola would convince me.

Setting Paco loose worried me. I had grown fond of him, but perhaps Osceola was right.

"Look, Paco, we should listen to Osceola," I told him. "You're growing up and you must learn to be on your own. If you don't, you'll never grow up to be a free raccoon."

Finally, I opened the cage and said good-bye to Paco, thinking he would leave. But next morning he was back in the cage. Juanito and I then decided to carry him off where he couldn't find us, so he'd learn to be free.

We took Paco away during one of those airboat rides Mike gave the tourists. I got off with Paco on a little island where, according to Mike, there had once been a village of fierce Indians.

Even though the Everglades was one big swamp, there were some higher, drier places, little islands known as hammocks. There, you wouldn't sink in the mud. It was on a hammock that I left Paco. I meant to leave him and return in a few days to check on him. As soon as Mike started the engine and we were ready to take off, poor Paco raised his snout and sniffed the air worriedly. It was as if he knew we were leaving him for good.

Just a day or so later, there was a big fire.

In the summer, it rains so much in the Everglades that everything floods and the place looks like one big lake. But during the winter it almost doesn't rain at all. Then, a fire can get started very easily: any small flame will set fire to the grass, which sets fire to a tree, and then another, and another and another, until everything burns. At night, sparks shoot up like fireworks. Sometimes the fires last for days. When they are over you see miles of burnt grass, ashes and scorched trees.

As soon as I saw fire on the island where we left Paco, I called Juanito.

"Wake up! Wake up! There's a big fire outside and we've got to save Paco!"

"*Ay, bendito!*" Juanito said, jumping into his pants.

Then, we called Tony. Silently, the three of us left the house and got on one of the airboats. We rowed quietly for a while, until we were far enough to start the engine without waking Mike. When we got to the island we found poor Paco in a circle of flames. He was dying of fright. I ran to rescue him.

"Don't go in, Kiki, don't be a fool!" Tony shouted.

But I jumped off anyway, and picked up Paco as fast as I could. On the way out, my shirt caught fire. I rolled on the ground. Tony and Juanito threw a wet blanket over me. But I got burnt anyway. When we got back Tony put oil and ice over my blisters. They hurt.

From then on, I kept Paco in his cage with the door open. But he never left it. The next time Osceola told me to set Paco free, I answered I couldn't force him to leave if he didn't want to.

"It isn't right for people to live caged up against their will; but it isn't right either for me to force Paco to live free against his will. Paco has the right to live wherever he wants!" I argued.

Osceola smiled and scratched his head. I told him that there were lots of people in the world who weren't free, like the Cubans who lived in Cuba, but they had no choice. At least, in Paco's case, the cage door was open. In the Cubans' case, it wasn't.

The next day after the fire, Mike got upset over the airboat. "Who the hell's been playing with my boat?"

I still don't know how he found out. Maybe it

was the way we tied it to the pier.

Mike was furious. He whipped out his belt and was on the point of giving us a thrashing when Mama stood between him and us, pleading:

"Don't you dare, Mike! They'll take the kids away from us!"

VIII
Adios, Everglades

In spite of fires, storms, ticks and alligator burgers, I would've liked to stay with Mike and Mama
in the Everglades. They didn't treat us badly after
all. On Saturdays they'd spend the whole day
watching TV and drinking beer till very late at
night. Next day, they'd sleep till noon, so we were
pretty much on our own. No one was after me to
do this or that or to go to school if I didn't want to.
Besides, I had learned a lot of things they didn't
teach in school.

I got to be the one who met the tourists and tell
them how dangerous the alligator was and how the
great Osceola was the only man around who could
handle it. At first everybody laughed at my Cuban
English, but they understood me.

Mike also taught me to pilot the airboat.
Whenever we flew over the sawgrass I imagined it
was really an airplane and it was loads of fun.

Being with Juanito, I had lost my fear of snakes
and I knew all the birds. It was fun to watch the
hard-headed kingfisher, especially when it tried to

land on the electric wires and tumbled forward. I also learned to recognize birds by their flight. Swallows knit the air like crazy. When a lot of them flew together, it seemed like all the sky was fluttering. Buzzards were ugly and ate rotten meat. But up in the sky they soared and glided beautifully without moving their wings. Migrating ducks flapped their wings like mad, as if in a hurry to leave the cold weather behind.

My favorite bird was the white heron. Near sunset you could see it roost on the tips of dwarf palms or on dry cypress trees, doing a balancing act. It craned its neck and stood still, as if posing for a picture. Sometimes it pulled up a leg, spread a wing and stayed that way, just like a ballerina.

When you come to the Everglades for the first

time, especially if it's raining, the place seems sad and ugly. But as time goes by, you get to like the flat land with its skinny trees and strange flowers crossed by canals that look like shimmering roads. I'll never forget the sunsets, when the sky turns red and the sun looks like a big ball of fire. Slowly it sinks till you can see only half of it, then a crescent, then nothing. Everything becomes peaceful and silent as the night sets in.

I would have stayed forever, but things started to go wrong and we were soon forced to leave.

It was mostly Tony's fault for falling in love with Tawami, a Miccosukee Indian girl. He began to act silly. He let his hair grow the same as hers and spent the whole day listening to music with his ears glued to a tiny transistor radio. He did nothing but think of her.

At that time, Mike had started buying all sorts of Indian souvenirs: belts, beads, change purses, stuffed baby alligators, and all the rest of the junk that tourists buy. Tawami pretended to deliver these things, but she did it only to see my brother. If two or three days went by and she didn't come, Tony would walk five miles to Tawami's village. He'd usually get Joshua to go along. I think he was scared of Tawami's brother, a big, short-tempered Indian who fished with a spear.

Indians didn't like their girls to go out with

white men; white folks liked it even less. But when
Mama warned Tony he would get in trouble, he
paid no attention. I suspect he and Tawami were
already going together.

One day I was playing with Paco when Juanito
came up in a hurry.

"*Ay, bendito!* We're in for it now! Tawami's
brother is here! And she's with Tony."

"Here?"

"Yes, under the tree, there!"

We ran to warn Tony but stopped short without
making a sound. Tony was kissing Tawami, just
like in the movies.

"Look out, Tony!" Juanito yelled.

Tony ignored us.

I whistled to Tony in alarm, the Lendián whistle.
Tawami managed to slip away, and that time nothing happened. But if we had stayed much longer at
Mike's, I'm sure Tony would have gotten in real
trouble.

Then came the worst. One Sunday at noon, the
welfare lady who had left us with Mike and Mama
showed up at the camp. She knocked hard on the
door and woke Mike. Mike got so mad, he told the
lady he was fed up. For the small change the government paid him to keep us there, he didn't have
to take her spying on him.

The lady turned stiff as a board and said:

"You're disgusting! Absolutely disgusting!"

which is what polite people say in this country when they don't like what they see.

I was anxious to be nice to her so she wouldn't jump to any conclusions, but Juanito later told me that I had messed up the whole thing.

When she asked me if we had gone to church, I answered truthfully.

"No, we never go."

The lady looked at me sternly. She was very Baptist.

"And what's that you're holding?" she asked.

I wondered if she was blind or just dumb. "A beer can."

"What? Mike gives you beer?"

"Not always. Only when it gets hot."

I thought the lady would faint.

"Call your brother, please," she said, recovering.

"He's not around. He went to see Tawami."

"Who's Tawami?"

"His girlfriend."

"For goodness' sake, the name sounds Indian!"

"It sure is. Tawami's a Miccosukee Indian. But don't worry, Ma'am, my brother Tony's got to break it off. Her brother told him that if he saw them together again, he'd kill him."

"Oh, dear! Oh, dear!" The lady lifted a hand to her head.

"Now you've done it! You've ruined it all!" said Juanito.

"Why?"

"First of all, even if we don't go to church on Sunday, we're supposed to. Secondly, in this country you're not allowed to drink beer before you're twenty-one. That's the law. And thirdly, you really blew it by telling her about Tawami. Now they will take you away, for sure. Why didn't you keep your big mouth shut, you idiot!"

Juanito had never talked to me like that. His eyes were full of tears. He turned his back to me and threw stones from the road into the canal.

I ran away so they couldn't find me when they came to get me. I took a few slices of bread and a couple of cans of beer and hid out in the same island where I'd left Paco. I made up my mind to stay there. But soon I heard police sirens and barking dogs. They were putting on a search for me, flashlights and all.

I thought things might turn worse if I didn't return, so I did. As I walked back, I saw a couple of policemen escorting Tony to a car.

"Where are you going, Tony? Where are they taking you?" I shouted.

I was all mixed up. I felt fear and anger.

"Where the devil have you been?" Tony asked me in Spanish.

"Listen carefully," he said. "The people at the agency have found a very nice place for you to stay; it's a doctor's home. Now get your things together and leave quietly."

"But I want to go with you, Tony!" I cried.

Tony gave me a hard look. "I'm sorry. You'll have to do what I say and you're going to behave."

"Forgive me, Tony. I won't do it again, I promise!"

He probably couldn't hear me because I was crying and the words just wouldn't come out right.

Tony patted me on the head. "Get your things, Kiki. I'll call you up whenever I can."

"I'm not going anywhere, dammit!" I snarled, kicking an empty gas can.

As they shoved me into the car, I kept yelling all the dirty words and phrases I had learned from Mike. I refused to say good-bye to Tony or to Osceola, to Mike or to Mama Jones. I did not say good-bye to anyone, not even to Paco. Juanito came closer, looking lonelier than ever. He raised his hand to wave. I punched the window and shouted:

"To hell with you! Damn you all!"

IX

My American Dad

For miles, the welfare lady sat in silence. I watched the Indian villages flying by, the sawgrass, the black people fishing off the bridges. When we reached the Miami city limits she asked me:

"Do you like to swim, Kiki?"

I turned my head away.

"Doctor Hamilton's home has a pool."

I shrugged, meaning I didn't care. Then, as I looked out the window, I started thinking about the future instead of the past. It helped a lot. I began to notice the cars. A passing Mercedes-Benz made me daydream about becoming an engineer and buying one with a convertible top. And a yacht, too. By the time we drove into Galloway Road, I was almost a millionaire.

Doctor Hamilton's home was in the middle of Coral Gables. The houses were big and surrounded with soft green lawns. All the streets were lined with shady banyan trees and poincianas full of orange-red blossoms.

Coral Gables was started by a man who was

crazy about Spain and Spaniards. The streets all have Spanish names or at least names that sound Spanish, like Samana or Calabra. Americans mispronounce the difficult names, like Hernando de Soto and Ponce de Leon, so if you hear them you can't even tell they're Spanish.

Coral Gables is full of mockingbirds brought from Cuba many years ago. A president of Cuba was a friend of the man who dreamed up Coral Gables, and he sent him a million pairs. The point is that they're Cuban mockingbirds. I liked that.

The inside of the doctor's home looked great: the furniture, the lamps, the big stairway. Now I realized how long it had been since I had last seen a nice home. It felt good to step on the rugs. There were windows everywhere looking out on trees and beyond, the swimming pool. It was so big, it looked like a lake. What a difference! I couldn't help remembering the Jones' camp in the Everglades.

Mrs. Hamilton met me with a big smile. She was slender and smelled good. I wondered how old she was. Here in the United States you can never really tell a woman's age. Juanito used to say that as soon as they begin to wrinkle, all rich women in this country get a special job done on their faces. A surgeon stretches and pulls their skin until all the wrinkles are ironed out. The scar from the operation is supposed to be behind the ear. But no matter how much I looked, I never saw a scar on Mrs. Hamilton. She couldn't have been too young, though, because she had a bent arthritic finger like my Aunt Juana, who wouldn't tell anyone her real age.

Since I had made up my mind not to believe in anyone anymore, I didn't trust Mrs. Hamilton. But soon I understood that I couldn't judge her the same way I had judged Mike Jones. The government wasn't paying her to look after me.

As soon as I came in, she called her daughters, Tessie and Julie, to introduce me. They were blonde and had blue eyes. Their clothes didn't go with the house; they were dressed like poor people with torn jeans. I understood later that many rich Americans don't like their clothes to look new. Tessie and Julie came up and said "Hi!" Then they asked their mother if my name was really Jesus, and started to laugh.

Mrs. Hamilton showed me to my room. We went up the carpeted stairs and when she opened the door I couldn't believe my eyes. There was a bed with a thick mattress, a color TV and shelves loaded with toys and games. You could see the swimming pool from the window. I was excited, but I didn't say a word. I didn't want Mrs. Hamilton to think I'd never had a room of my own before.

"Tomorrow we'll get you a bathing suit and new school clothes," she said.

My Cuban clothes were worn-out, too old and too small for me. I had no underwear left, but I said nothing because I didn't want her to think I was really poor.

Doctor Hamilton arrived around six. He was tall and thin. His eyes were blue and he had a kind face. He asked me if all my ancestors were Cuban. Then he told me he was mostly Irish. Here, no one's grandparents seem to be from the U.S.A. They're all from another country like England, Germany, Poland or Italy. After a while they learn to speak English with an American accent. Then, they become Americans and it doesn't really matter where anyone comes from. Some even change their names to make them sound more American. I'm never going to change my name, even if it's Jesús, even if it's unusual, and even if it's mispronounced.

Doctor Hamilton's hair was black with streaks of grey around his forehead and around his ears. He didn't tint it either. When they got to Miami, many older Cuban men colored their hair to look younger. They thought it was hard to get a job if you looked old.

You could tell Doctor Hamilton was a doctor. He looked so clean and he always wore a white coat down to his knees. He moved his hands slowly and carefully. Probably because he was an eye doctor, Doctor Hamilton looked at people straight in the eye, I guess to check whether or not they were nearsighted. Or maybe he was like Tata. Just by looking at you, she could tell whether or not you were lying.

He shook my hand when he arrived. He seemed to be listening to me before I even said the first word. Some people look at you, but you know they're not really listening. And if they do listen, they don't give a damn about what you're saying. Not Doctor Hamilton; he saw and heard. He asked me a lot of questions about Havana and about my family. I hadn't talked about my parents in a long time. I told him my father had taught me to play baseball. I wanted to talk about Tony, but I couldn't; it hurt too much. The doctor told me that if I wanted to I could call him John. He also said that he loved Spanish. He was learning it because many of his elderly patients were Cuban.

"Why don't you and I speak in Spanish?" he asked. "That way I can practice."

I couldn't believe my ears! For a long time now, all I had heard was "Don't speak Spanish." My eyes are green and my hair light, so everyone spoke to me in English and thought I was American.

At eight o'clock that night we ate in the large dining room. The table was set with a real tablecloth and napkins. Mrs. Hamilton served steaks. It was hard for me to use a knife again. The only meat I'd eaten lately was hot dogs and alligator hamburgers. Now, along with the steak, I had all the French fries I wanted, and after, ice cream topped with hot chocolate syrup.

Tessie and Julie looked at me and giggled. I didn't know why. The only thing I shouldn't have done was to scoop up with my spoon the ice cream that had dripped on my shirt.

After supper, the Doctor went to his library to read. I stayed and watched TV with Mrs. Hamilton and the girls. They were not my family, I knew, but they almost felt like it. At ten we were told to go to bed. Doctor Hamilton and I shook hands and said good night.

Mrs. Hamilton followed me upstairs and handed me some pajamas. They were so new they still had the store tags on them. She showed me the bathroom, gave me brand new towels, and turned on the water. She told me to get in. I stared. In Cuba nobody ever took a bath right after a meal. It could make you sick and you could even die. At least that's what our grandmother used to say. When we went to the beach, mother would never let us go in the water till at least three hours after eating.

"Go ahead," Mrs. Hamilton insisted. "You'll feel great after a shower."

I gulped, not knowing how to explain my fear.

To make her understand, I made a face, twisted my
mouth and pointed to the shower, saying
"Dangerous, dangerous."

Mrs. Hamilton probably thought I was a dirtball
who hated baths. She scolded me and wagged her
index finger in the air. She pointed at the shower
again and closed the door behind her.

I washed my face and hands carefully, and
passed a damp towel all over my body. I certainly
didn't want to die in such a beautiful house, with
such a beautiful swimming pool and all those great
steaks! How could Mrs. Hamilton want me to risk
my life after being so nice? These American *grin-
gos,* as Juanito used to call them, were strange people!

I couldn't help it: I'd have to fool Mrs.
Hamilton. I opened the shower head full force so
she would think I was really using it. Then I
stepped out of the bathroom and got into bed in my
new pajamas. The bed felt like a cloud compared
to the bunk I had slept in at the Jones'.

I was about to fall asleep when the doctor came
in. He looked at me tenderly, as he would've
looked at the son he didn't have. Putting his hand
on my forehead and turning out the light, he said,
"Good night, son," and was gone.

I tried to say "Good night, Dad (as his daughters
called him)," but instead I said: "Good night, sir."

The next day at breakfast, they offered me a white soupy cereal and I turned it down. Instead, they gave me eggs with bacon, toast and milk. I hadn't eaten so much in a long time.

After breakfast, Doctor Hamilton took me to a large public school. He went with me to see the principal. She was very tall and thin and she wore a wig. They both shook hands and looked at me, as if I was some sort of insect. Then, forcing a smile, she put a hand on my shoulder. She was trying to act nice in front of the doctor.

There were plenty of Cuban kids in the school who had their mothers and fathers here and not in Cuba, like mine. Very soon we all became friends. Some Americans were friendly, but others called me the "new spic" and laughed at me.

My first teacher was not an American but an English lady by the name of Mrs. Chipley. She always wore flowery print dresses and shoes with laces. She had been teaching for a long, long time and she would creep through the lessons, as if we were all dumb. When she asked my name and I said Jesús Lendián, she didn't answer me directly, but the rest of the day she called me Jimmy.

I reminded her that my name was Jesús. She replied:

"Yes, yes, but here in class we'll call you Jimmy."

I made up my mind not to answer when she called me Jimmy because I didn't want my name changed.

"Look, *chico,* don't take it so hard," a classmate from Spain advised me. "I'm in worse shape than you are. My last name is Iruretagoyena. They can't even begin to pronounce it! Whenever I see the teacher stop and look twice at the list, I know it's my name coming up. 'Ih-ru-ray...' and I say 'here' right away! And think of Conchita! Her name is Immaculate Conception!"

He couldn't convince me. I was named Jesús after my father; Andres, after an uncle who was a pilot; and *de la Caridad* after the Cuban patron saint. Nobody, but nobody, was going to change my name—Jesús Andres de la Caridad Lendián y Gómez!

Back home, I spoke to the doctor in Spanish about my name problem.

"The teacher says they'll have to call me Jimmy, but my name is Jesús and..."

Doctor Hamilton laughed and said that the teacher knew nothing about Spanish names. The doctor explained, in his slow and careful Spanish, that people in the United States took their religion seriously. If they were Catholics, they were very Catholic. If they were Jewish or Baptist, they were very, very Jewish or very, very Baptist. He asked me if I knew the Ten Commandments.

I recited the ones I could remember.

"Do you recall the one that says, 'Thou shall not take the name of the Lord in vain?'"

That one had skipped my mind, but I couldn't see the connection between the Ten Commandments and the teacher calling me Jimmy.

"Look," the doctor said, "people in Spanish-speaking countries name their children Jesús in memory of Jesus Christ. But here, to say 'Jesus' is to swear. It sounds bad. And if you say 'Jesus Christ!' it sounds even worse. People say that only when they're angry. It's, well, profanity, a bad word, like saying *coño* in Spanish. Now, just suppose you were an American in Cuba and *Coño* was your name, what then?"

I wanted to laugh when I heard the doctor say *coño*, but I didn't so he wouldn't think I was making fun of his Spanish.

"Perhaps we could straighten out the problem by having the teacher call you Hay-Soose, the way it's pronounced in Spanish, and not Jesus in English. It doesn't sound bad that way, does it?"

I agreed with him and that was the end of the problem—until a few days later.

I was given some forms to fill out with my name, address, telephone number and so on. One of the blank spaces was for my race. I wrote down white. The teacher looked at the form, crossed out white and wrote *Cuban* instead. That bothered me.

"Listen, teacher, Cuban is not a race; it just means I'm from Cuba, and I am a white Cuban."

"I know, Hay-Soose, but here you write Cuban where it says race."

The next time I saw the school counselor, I told her about it. She laughed because she was Cuban, too.

"You're right, Jesús," she said. "We do it to make things easier. Cubans are not used to being asked their racial background. To avoid any misunderstandings, school officials have come up with the Cuban race."

So it turned out that I, and Chang, the Chinese-Cuban, and black Orestes, my classmate, were all part of the Cuban race. How about that?

When I told the doctor, he laughed and remarked:

"We've come a long way in America, Jesús, but there are still a lot of useless prejudices around. Perhaps, since our country is a democracy, you can help change things for the better.

"I didn't wait to grow up to fight prejudice," the doctor went on. "Years ago, when I was still in school up north, changes took place in our district that brought in black children for the first time to our school. Most of my schoolmates and their parents objected, but I stuck up for the black children's right to come to our school. I even protected a scared black girl with pigtails—her name was Lucy—from the bigger white children who stood at the door calling her names. Looking after Lucy made me feel better inside."

"I'm Cuban," I said.

"I know. We still have some prejudices against Hispanics, too. Perhaps you can help correct that."

Frankly, I didn't know how.

One evening, Doctor and Mrs. Hamilton went out to dinner. I stayed home watching TV with Julie and Tessie. At ten o'clock, Julie turned on a show about cowboys.

I sat there watching till I looked at Tessie. She was sitting close to me, her hair was like gold and it fell softly on her shoulders. She smelled so nice! Like jasmine. I could hear her breathing. Suddenly, I felt something funny in my stomach and I don't know what came over me. I turned Tessie's face towards me and kissed her.

Just then, Julie, who had gone to the kitchen to get popcorn, walked in and started yelling at me.

"I'll tell Dad, as soon as he comes home! I'll tell him! You're the same as all Latins! You are all macho men! You look at girls walk! You tell them things even if you don't know them!"

"That's a Cuban custom! Besides, we only say

nice things, like doll or beautiful."

"You said it! It's a Cuban custom. But this is America and I'm American and I won't have you kissing my sister!"

"North America!" I corrected her.

"It's all the same."

"No, it isn't, because there's a North and a South America."

"When one says America," Julie added, "everybody knows that it means the United States, dummy."

"You're both dummies if you know only what's here and believe that here is all that matters."

She was so mad, I wondered if it was because I had kissed her sister and not her.

"You have to become American and act like an American! The sooner the better!"

I decided to go upstairs; there was no way to make Julie understand how I felt. I closed the door and got into bed. My head was spinning. I was confused. All of a sudden a thought struck me. I sat up in bed. *¡Ay, bendito!* I remembered what Juanito said when we caught Tony kissing Tawami. How would Doctor Hamilton take it if he caught me kissing Tessie?

I couldn't sleep, and when I did, I had a nightmare. Doctor Hamilton was kicking me out of the house, Tessie was breaking out in laughter, and some cops were forcing me into a patrol car. I tried to run away but my feet wouldn't obey me.

Next morning at breakfast I couldn't look at anybody straight in the eye. Mrs. Hamilton asked me if I was sick. Julie didn't say anything and Tessie looked at me with no hard feelings. She even smiled at me.

I decided I would never kiss her again. Not now, anyway. My cousin Conchita always said she wouldn't let any man kiss her but her boyfriend. My mother and my grandmother had taught me to be a *caballero*, a gentleman. Well, I really hadn't been one. Some day I would ask Tessie to be my girlfriend and then I would marry her.

X

I'm Becoming American, But...

I didn't kiss Tessie again, but still she had a lot
to do with improving my baseball. I was on the
school team and we went all the way to the local
championship game. One day I was lucky enough
to hit a homer with the bases loaded. My team won
the game and suddenly I became very popular.
They even put my picture in the school newspaper.
Everybody said "Hi, Kiki!" when they met me, and
Tessie looked at me with a proud look in her eyes.

This started me thinking that it might be better
for me to become American all the way. I tried to
get rid of all traces of my Cuban accent.
Sometimes I wouldn't answer when someone
spoke to me in Spanish.

A lot of non-Cuban kids became my friends.
Having a swimming pool and nice house made it
easy to make new friends. Or maybe it was Doctor
Hamilton's Mercedes-Benz. People just don't treat
a Cuban in an old Cadillac the same way they do a
Cuban in a Mercedes-Benz. Living at the
Hamiltons' changed my ways, to the point that

sometimes other Cubans' behavior embarrassed me, especially if they seemed ignorant. Like Cachita, a Cuban lady that Mrs. Hamilton hired to do housework. Cachita was thrilled to have another Cuban in the house. I tried to stay away from her not because she was a Cuban, but because she was plain dumb.

She kept saying that there were Russian missiles in Cuba and that Castro—whom she called The Horse, as Cubans do—would attack the United States.

"Kiki, do you know how they hid those missiles in Cuba?"

"How?"

"With mantles—you know, like cloaks."

"Mantles? Cloaks? What do you mean, Cachita?"

"Kiki, didn't they say they had *dismantled* the Russian missiles?"

It wasn't just people like Cachita that made it hard for Americans to understand Cubans. We were different and sometimes we acted differently. In the mixed neighborhoods in southwest Miami, some Americans were driven away by our loud talk on the streets, not to mention the big family gatherings to eat roast pork.

One day Doctor Hamilton took me to Eighth Street, right in the heart of what is known as Little

Havana, where you can get everything we used to have in Cuba. You can eat in Spanish, buy clothes in Spanish, even die in Spanish.

There are things that didn't even exist in Cuba, like the voodoo shops known as *botanicas*, where you can buy magic herbs and spices and even some weird cans of spray. The label promises that if you used it in your house while saying the prayer written on it, you would get rid of all the evil spirits and chase away bad luck. To me it was no worse, after all, than Osceola's belief in little men who lived underground. Besides, except for Tata, no one in my family believed in voodoo.

Dr. Hamilton wanted some Cuban guava pastry and black Cuban coffee, so we went into a Cuban cafeteria and sat at the counter next to a policeman. When the policeman ordered a Coke, they served him one with a fly swimming in it. He signaled to the plump Cuban waitress with dyed hair and long nails.

She walked over to his place on the counter and he politely explained in English that there was a fly in his Coke.

When he realized he wasn't being understood, the policeman made a buzzing sound with his lips and flapped his hands like wings, pointing at the glass.

"Hey, doll," she called in Spanish to another

waitress, "Come and see what this *Americano* wants. He's acting very queer and I'm taking no insults from anyone."

Patiently, the cop repeated his fly-in-the-Coke act to the second waitress.

"I'm sorry, *señor*," she said in Spanish. "It's not our fault if the Coke has no gas."

The cop looked around. "Ain't there somebody in this joint who speaks English?" he demanded angrily.

After all, this was the U.S.A.

After that I made a big effort to show the Hamiltons that Cubans were smart. I began to study as I never had before and got straight A's. The Hamiltons were so pleased with me that on my birthday they gave me a boat to race at the club. I was already calling them Mom and Dad.

Dad was very fond of sailing. He said he'd rather listen to the wind than to the sound of TV or people talking. On Sundays, the two of us would go fishing, or pretended to, because if the fish were small, Dad would toss them back into the water. With Dad I also learned to snorkel, a word I never knew in Spanish.

It was always quiet under the sea. The plants moved in slow motion and the sunlight drew wavy lines on the sandy bottom. There were yellow fish with blue stripes, others with black stripes, and still

others that looked like silver streaks. Some came up to you and stared. "Who are you?" they seemed to wonder. There were seahorses and lobsters and octopi (or is it octopuses?) dancing on their tentacles. The white corals looked like fans. There were tiny prairies where grasses swayed as if they were being blown by an undersea breeze.

I began to feel that Dad was my real father and that my life with him would last forever. I realized that in many ways I wasn't as Cuban as before. I didn't even miss fried plantains. I still liked black beans, but not the way I used to. Mom got the recipe from a friend, and on my twelfth birthday she made black beans. They turned out greyish-looking and hard as rocks. But I didn't want to hurt her feelings, so I never told her how awful they tasted. She was so glad, she started making them for me every Friday!

So much time had gone by that I'd nearly forgotten my parents' faces. Besides, I never heard from them. Dad Hamilton said it was not their fault, but rather the mail in Cuba. Every month he made me write them a letter, but I couldn't think of anything to say. Besides, they weren't going to understand what I was writing about because things in the U.S.A. were so different. I never saw Tony, either, although he did call now and then. Gradually I got used to the idea that I would never see my family again. What really mattered was that I had made up my mind to keep what was mine now.

One Halloween, when I was dressed up as a ghost, Dad called me into his study. He said he had something very important to tell me.

I thought it would be a matter of a minute or two, so I didn't even take off my mask. But Dad sat down in his armchair, reached for his pipe, lit it very calmly, blew out the match, and watched the smoke drift away in curls. Finally, his eyes met mine.

"Jesús (he did pronounce it Hay-soose), we love you like a son, and this house will always be your home."

That's it, I thought. Now they'll send me to Matecumbe, for sure.

I didn't want him to say it because then it would hurt more, so I interrupted him.

"Where are they sending me now?"

He looked surprised. "No, that's not it, son. They called to tell us that your parents have just arrived from Cuba and they want to see you right away."

I said what was in my heart. "They should have stayed there!"

When Dad asked me, "Just what are you saying, son?" I hugged him, in tears.

"I don't want to leave! I love you so much, Dad!"

He put his arms around me, too. But then let go.

"They're your parents, Jesús, and if they want you with them, you'll have to go."

I snapped back in anger:

"No, I don't! Why did they lie and send me here alone? If they stayed in Cuba it was because the house and the farm meant more to them than my brother and me. Besides, I hardly remember them anyway!"

It crossed my mind—but I didn't say it—that all Cubans arrived penniless and that I wasn't about to go through that all over again. I remembered how hungry I had been! So, then, at the top of my voice, I shouted:

"I don't ever want to see my father and mother again!"

In a steady voice Dad said, "Take off your costume and wash your face; your parents are about to arrive."

As I was leaving, he added, "I think you're being unfair. They did what they considered best for you. I want you to be there waiting for them, and be nice."

I dressed and sat down to wait at the doorway. My mind was made up not to go with them, and if they forced me to, I'd run away where they'd never be able to find me.

An old battered Plymouth stopped in the driveway. The doors swung open. I looked. A lady came running towards me shouting, "Kiki, my son!"

Behind her, I could see a man that looked a lot like my father, only much older. Then I heard a voice calling, "Kiki! Kiki!"

It was Tony. Suddenly, time had stood still. My heart skipped a few beats.

"Tony! Tony!" The four of us embraced, crying.

XI

Who Am I?

But we didn't live happily ever after. Not quite. We had many problems. I could hardly remember what it was like to live with my real parents. Here in the U.S.A., I had been on my own and grown more independent. All of a sudden my real father was ordering me to obey every rule, no questions asked.

Out of pride, Papa accepted Dad's money as a loan only, and then just five hundred dollars. On that money, all we could rent was a little house in Hialeah. My parents were very happy, but I felt awful. I would have to get my things together and say good-bye to the Hamiltons. And even though I knew I could see them again, I realized it would never be the same as before.

To make matters worse, instead of my nice big bed, I had to sleep on a thin mattress placed on top of a worn-out box spring. Instead of the polished chest of drawers, a couple of wooden crates would have to do to put my clothes away. Our second-hand refrigerator needed constant defrosting to keep it from becoming an iceberg inside. The living room furniture came from the flea market. Our china was a jumble of odd pieces from broken sets. So was our flatware: spoons and forks and knives, all discolored and bent out of shape. For transportation, Papa got a 1950-something Cadillac that made a terrible noise when he finally got it started.

Papa found a discarded TV set in a junk pile. He spent a week fixing it up. On top of it Mama placed a porcelain elephant and a couple of ashtrays, all sitting on a woven scarf.

All this turned out to be an important lesson for me: it's harder to learn to be poor than to learn to be rich. I was definitely on my way down.

Every time Conchita, one of Mama's friends, showed up with a bundle of old clothing, Mama would cry:

"Look, Papa! A silk blouse! It looks new! And look! Stockings! Sheets, too! Oh, how we needed them! And there's more! Look! A suit! A whole suit! I bet it'll fit you!"

Everything looked faded, crushed and wrinkled. But my mother took everything anyway, thankfully, beaming with joy. For me, they were hand-me-downs. I had grown spoiled at the Hamilton's and I was embarrassed every time I had to wear used clothes. I kept my feelings to myself, though. Mama was like Alice in Wonderland. She had spent many days in Cuba standing in long lines just to buy a handkerchief or a pair of stockings that would get runs on the first wearing. She was so anxious to decorate our new home, putting plastic flowers here and little curtains there. She kept things neat and shiny and she was always happily making plans for the future. She saved the green stamps that they gave her at the supermarket. It took her forever to collect enough stamps to get an iron.

Before she finally got a steady job at a factory, Mama did all kinds of odd jobs to make ends meet. She baked guava pastries to sell, she sewed, she did a lot of baby-sitting—anything that would bring in a little money. I never heard her complain, as many Cubans do, over what was lost in Cuba. On the contrary, she was always looking around and saying:

"Oh, sometimes I think I'm dreaming! All the family together again!"

Mama got into the funny habit of saving empty jars. "Don't throw them away!" she'd say. "Do you know what your grandmother in Cuba would give for a jar like this?" We ended up having all kinds of jars coming out of every corner of the house.

She also saved leftovers. She would serve them until they had disappeared completely. That meant we ate the same food for a couple of days straight.

If I complained, she'd say, "Do you realize that in Cuba you could only get two ounces of meat each week? Do you know you don't get any milk unless you're under five or over sixty?"

I can't say I felt as close to Papa. He was a lot more serious than Mama. He had been a lawyer in Cuba, but what could a Cuban lawyer do in Miami, especially if he didn't speak English? He managed to get a job at a restaurant, but he didn't know how to be a waiter, and it made him grouchy. Papa picked on me now that Tony worked days and studied at night.

"Kiki, put on your shoes. Kiki, you need a haircut." And on and on.

One day I couldn't take it anymore and I said, "At Dad's house I didn't wear any shoes if I didn't want to and I'd cut my hair whenever I felt like it."

"You said it, at Dad's, but not here. Here you'll put your shoes on and get your hair cut when I say so."

He got very angry when I spoke to him in English.

"Say it in Spanish, Kiki!"

And I'd answer, "Skip it, it's not that important."

Sometimes I did it to bother him, but sometimes it was just easier for me to say things in English.

And usually, he would insist, "Say it again, in Spanish."

"But it's not that important."

"Yes, it is. We will always speak Spanish in this house."

Then Papa decided I needed to learn Spanish grammar and Cuban history. He gave me lessons before he left for his new job as a mechanic. I had to be up early each morning, still sleepy, to hear him go on and on about Cuban patriots like Marti and Maceo and the Cuban wars of independence. No people have fought harder or longer for their freedom than Cubans, he would add proudly.

Then he would order me to do homework in Spanish.

Papa also got it into his head that American football was too rough. When I was picked to be on the school team, he said:

"No, Kiki, forget it! Now, if it were soccer..."

"Everybody here plays American football," I replied.

"Sure, and that's why so many young people get hurt. Besides those football players look like a bunch of stupid monsters. No wonder they sent me that release form to sign and the insurance papers!"

"Papa, in this country you have to sign releases and take out insurance to do anything!"

"That may be true, but as far as I'm concerned, you can play baseball, swim, or even row. But football is out!"

"But, Papa..."

"Don't argue, Kiki. You're not playing football and that's that."

I got angry and said:

"Cigarettes cause cancer. They are a lot worse than football and yet you smoke all day long."

I turned around and left him alone, struggling for words.

We always had company. Everyone kissed and hugged everyone else. It took forever to say "hello" and "good-bye." All the old ladies would take a look at me, and tell me how much I'd grown. Then they'd all begin to talk out loud at the same time, and always about politics. I don't know why, but they always ended up discussing whether or not Fidel Castro had always been a communist. Usually someone shouted:

"No doubt about it! And I should know—we were classmates."

"That's not true! He came to this country hoping that the American Congress would help him and he was turned down!"

"That's a lie! He's always been more of a communist than Stalin himself!"

My father and his friends could go on like this for hours. But if they started with "Do you remember?" it was even worse.

"Do you remember Old Man Chano? And what

about that kid, the one they called Big Baby? And
Lolita Farto?" Since these names made them laugh,
I thought I'd hear some funny stories. But no: Old
Man Chano died; Big Baby was sentenced to
twenty years; and Lolita, who had joined the mili-
tia, was later arrested. Nothing but tragedy!

One evening, some of our old neighbors from
Havana came over and Papa made me stay home.
There was going to be a Miami Dolphins game, so
I turned on the TV.

Papa ordered, "Turn it down, Kiki!" Then he
said to his friends, "These kids are deaf; they turn
that thing on as high as it'll go. And the music! It
drives you crazy! What's more, they don't care if
there's a conversation going. You ask them nicely
to keep it low and they don't even answer!"

I lowered the volume, but they were talking so
loud I couldn't hear the announcer call the plays.
And do you know what they were talking about?
Street vendors! What did the guy who sold tamales
in Havana actually say as he walked the streets trying to peddle his stuff? Was it "They're hot!
They're hot!" or "They're steaming!"? How did the
pastry peddler's song go? "Come and get 'em,
come and get 'em! They're delicious!"

Then they ended up talking about long-gone
Havana trolley cars and their routes.

"Beach to Central Station," one of them said.

As if answering a riddle, a second one added:

"That one ran along Twenty-third Street, then into Almendares and after several more stops, the terminal."

It could have been Chinese, for all I understood, but to them it was one big laugh.

And then the Dolphins scored!

"Man, oh man! Way to go!" I yelled.

"Keep quiet!" Papa thundered back. "What's the matter with you?"

"Ahhh, shit!"

One of the neighbors turned to my father, "That word! I hear it from my kids every two minutes!"

"And what does it mean?"

"*Mierda*, man, *mierda*," he answered staring at the floor sadly.

Papa got up and turned off the TV, with the score tied at fourteen and just a minute left to play.

I ran to my room and slammed the door. That was it! What the hell! My parents and I couldn't understand each other. We didn't like the same things; we didn't even speak the same language anymore!

"I'm leaving!" I told myself. "I'm going to be me."

I sat on the edge of the bed. I was all mixed up inside. I had been like that for a long time. I couldn't tell whether I was Cuban, American, both or nothing at all! I didn't like some of the things Cubans did, but I didn't like some of the things Americans did, either. Sometimes I was tempted to take off for Alaska. Sometimes I wanted to return to Cuba. I talked half in English, half in Spanish. If they played the American National Anthem, I'd get goose bumps. But if they played the Cuban Anthem, I'd get a knot in my throat. My parents were to blame. Why did they send me away from Cuba? Why didn't they just leave me there? Or why hadn't they stayed there themselves, so I'd be free to be one thing or the other, and not this mess I couldn't figure out?

It was very late when I finally looked at my watch, so I decided to leave first thing in the morning.

As I left the room that morning, I noticed my father sitting in an armchair, with the ashtray next to him full of cigarette butts. He called me over.

"Look, Kiki, after everybody left last night I called Doctor Hamilton."

"Dad?"

"Yes."

"What for?"

"Sit down."

He spoke slowly, as if trying hard to get himself across.

"Kiki, we spent four long years away from you.

We love you and we don't want to lose you, but if
you feel more comfortable with the Hamiltons, if
you understand them better, well, we can't do anything about it. We've tried! So, go! The doctor says
he wants to see you."

His eyes were full of sadness. He reminded me
of myself. It seemed as if we had traded places and
now he was my son.

To show him, once and for all, that I was my
own boss I went back to my room and began to
pack.

Mama entered and asked, "What are you doing?"

"I'm going to live with Dad Hamilton."

"Says who?"

"Me!"

For a second my mother looked as if she was
going to break down, not knowing what to do, but
suddenly she snatched away the shirt I was folding:

"No, sir, you're staying right here, you understand? Right here! We're your family. For better or
worse, we're your real family! I'm your mother
and I love you. If we have to face hard times, we'll
face them together. If we have to adjust to life
here, we will. That's it!"

Then she began to weep and sat down on the
bed. She spoke in a lower tone:

"I know you've had a hard time. So have we.
But there'll be a change: everything changes. I'm

going to learn English and your father's going to find out what American football is all about because you're going to teach him. We'll try. We'll all try. That's the important thing, trying. Besides, you're a Cuban, son. You were born in Cuba and your parents, like it or not, are Cubans, too. And listen well: your roots are in Cuba and your name is Jesús Lendián y Gómez. And nobody's taking that Gómez from you because it's in your blood. Accept your roots, Kiki, and be proud of what God made you. There's nothing worse than wanting to be what you're not. We have to stick together, fight it out and not give up! Right?"

I nodded slowly, not because of what she said but because of the truth that filled her eyes.

"Right," I said.

✳ ✳ ✳

The sun is burning mercilessly down on the docks. It has been eighteen years since I came to the United States with my brother and cousins. Now at the age of 27, I'm standing on the dock at Key West. Two weeks ago, 10,000 Cubans surged into the Peruvian Embassy in Havana demanding to leave Cuba. Fidel declared that anyone who wanted to leave by boat could do so from the port of Mariel. I am one of the volunteers waiting for

the hundreds of boats arriving from Cuba.

As the boats draw near the shore, the Cubans jump out. Some get down on their knees and kiss the ground.

They look like stumbling shadows, dark and hungry, wondering about the future, wondering if they will ever again see their parents, their brothers and sisters left behind in Cuba. All they have are the clothes on their backs, yet they walk bravely out of the past and into the unknown.

A line soon forms before me: men, women, children, old folks. They look tired, hungry and confused. I can't help thinking about my own arrival. I see myself marching among them, not as I am now, but as the lonely kid who took his trip to freedom eighteen years ago. I want to tell them many things. I want to tell them all that has been done to get them here: how some people have mortgaged their homes to rent or buy the boats on which they have come; how we have collected food, clothing and medicine for them; how a nice warm meal is waiting for them inside the building, and even an image of our Cuban patron saint; how on the rooftop of that same building, somebody with unsinkable Cuban wit had written:

"WILL THE LAST CUBAN LEAVING CUBA, PLEASE TURN OFF THE LIGHTS?"

But I just look at them and I can't speak. I stretch out my arm and place my hand on the head of a boy sent to freedom without his parents, like me.

"*Bienvenido, hermanito,* Welcome, little brother."

Afterword

Between January 15, 1961 and October 26, 1962, a period of 21 months, some 14,000 unaccompanied Cuban children entered the United States. Instead of a visa stamped in a Cuban passport by a U. S. Consular official, each carried, along with their passport, a letter signed by me, as the Executive Director of the Catholic Welfare Bureau in Miami. This was the "visa waiver," mentioned in this story. The Consulate in Havana had been closed on January 3, 1961, and there was no way to get a visa to enter the United States. The "visa waiver" ended when all commercial flights between Cuba and the United States were suspended because of the Missile Crisis.

The U. S. Department of State granted me the authority to sign these letters because our agency had agreed earlier to resettle in the United States unaccompanied minors from Cuba. The children who came with "visa waivers" were from all sectors of Cuban society. They were from all parts of the island. They represented every ethnic group and religious tradition on the island nation. The majority were teenage boys, followed by teenage girls. About twenty percent were children under twelve.

Upon arrival in Miami, about fifty percent went with relatives, like the hero of this story. The others were placed in transit shelters. One of these was Camp Matecumbe where his cousins were placed. For all of them it was a traumatic experience. But the children showed remarkable resilience and coped very well with the loss of family, a new culture and language. The story is well told and reflects the experiences of these youngsters who are now entering middle age, with children and grandchildren of their own.

From the beginning, the two most common questions asked were: "What motivated their parents to do it?" and "How did they do it?" The motivation was simple. They wanted to save their children from communist indoctrination. How they did it was more complex. The majority were helped by a small group of dedicated persons led by Ramon Grau Alsina and his sister Polita. With the help of sympathizers in foreign embassies, they maintained contact with me in Miami. Lists of names and birth dates came to me and I sent back the "visa waivers" and U. S. money orders needed to purchase the airline tickets. Similar correspondence was maintained with other groups throughout the island.

The initial hope was that the families would be reunited in a free Cuba. This hope faded after the failure of the Bay of Pigs invasion. Parents themselves began to make plans to leave the island. However, few made it until 1966, when the Freedom flights began to operate between Varadero Beach and Miami. In a few months, the vast majority were once again with their families. The conflicts experienced by Jesús were not uncommon, and this is perhaps the most important part of the story for me. Some parents never made it.

Every effort was made to keep this operation secret. The Miami press corps cooperated in this effort and named the program "Operation Pedro Pan." In 1964, Ramon and his sister, Polita, were arrested in Cuba and sentenced to long prison terms. Polita was released as a result of an appeal I made to Fidel Castro in 1978. Ramon was released in 1986 in response to an appeal by the U. S. Catholic Conference of Bishops. As he left prison, a Cuban official cursed him saying that they should have executed him 24 years before for what he had done to the youth of Cuba.

Today, these same youth are to be found in every walk of life, in Miami and throughout the hemisphere. They represent the best in Cuban life in exile and the hope of a free Cuba in the not too distant future. This is the real reward for Ramon, Polita, the countless others, both Cuban and American, for all of us who made it happen. Hilda Perera has captured in her story the essence of what happened thirty years ago.

But this story has an appeal beyond the Cuban-American experience. During the past sixty years there have been many "Operations Pedro Pan." I think of the Basque children sent to England and France during the Spanish Civil War. Spanish children sent to Russia and Mexico at the end of the war. Jewish children from Germany in foster homes in England. English children sent to the U. S. during the Blitz in 1940, I think of the Jewish children who survived the Holocaust. I think of the Hungarian Freedom fighters, teenagers who made it to the U. S. to escape the Soviet tanks. I think of the Indo-Chinese. I think of the Mozambique children I saw last year in Zimbabwe. Everywhere, there are refugees, there are children separated from their families. Hilda Perera's Kiki represents them all.

Monsignor Bryan O. Walsh